MICHAEL DAHL'S
REALLY SCARY STORIES

Raintree is an imprint of Capstone Global Library Limited, a company
incorporated in England and Wales having its registered office at
264 Banbury Road, Oxford, OX2 7DY — Registered company number: 6695582

www.raintree.co.uk
myorders@raintree.co.uk

Text © Capstone Global Library Limited 2018

The moral rights of the proprietor have been asserted.

Edited by Eliza Leahy
Designed by Tracy McCabe
Original illustrations © Capstone 2017
Illustrated by Xavier Bonet
Image Credits: Shutterstock: Dmitry Natashin, black box design element
Production by Kathy McColley
Printed and bound in China.

ISBN 978 1 4747 4418 8
21 20 19 18 17
10 9 8 7 6 5 4 3 2 1

British Library Cataloguing in Publication Data
A full catalogue record for this book is available from the British Library.

Acknowledgements
Every effort has been made to contact copyright holders of material
reproduced in this book. Any omissions will be rectified in subsequent
printings if notice is given to the publisher.

All the internet addresses (URLs) given in this book were valid at the time
of going to press. However, due to the dynamic nature of the internet, some
addresses may have changed, or sites may have changed or ceased to exist
since publication. While the author and publisher regret any inconvenience
this may cause readers, no responsibility for any such changes can be
accepted by either the author or the publisher.

SHADOW SHOES
AND OTHER SCARY TALES

By Michael Dahl

Illustrated by
Xavier Bonet

raintree
a Capstone company — publishers for children

CONTENTS

Dear Reader,

One night, I stepped outside to get some fresh air. It was a dark, moonless December night in Minnesota, USA. The winter had been warmer than average – no snow on the ground and leaves were still clinging to the trees.

Someone was standing across the street and appeared to be staring at me. The figure stood in the alley across from my house, next to a row of bushes. The figure was dark. I couldn't see its face or even the colour of its clothes.

Silently, smoothly, the figure glided sideways, then disappeared behind the bushes. I raced over to the alley (I know, awful idea), and in mere seconds the figure had gone. Vanished!

I KNOW WHAT I SAW, but I don't let it scare me.

Strange figures and shadows hide in the stories of this book, staring out at you.

Be brave – stare right back!

Michael Dahl

STUCK

For Raj and his cousins, it was the day *after* Halloween that scared them.

Clean-up day.

All the Halloween decorations had to be taken down, wiped off, pulled apart, packed up and hauled away. Every last glow-in-the dark skeleton, zombie figure and witch's cauldron. When it came to plastic pumpkins alone, there were forty-three to collect, clean and pack away.

"So. Many. Decorations," Raj moaned.

"You didn't complain yesterday when you were collecting sweets and scaring your cousins," said Uncle Dan.

Raj's aunt and uncle hosted a huge Halloween party every year at their modern home at the edge of town. Behind their house stood a much older building. The building made the perfect haunted mansion. Even before the decorations had been added, it looked like the set of a horror film. Doors hung open on broken hinges. Ceiling and wall lamps were coated with thick dust. Spider webs and cobwebs had created their own kingdom. They invaded every corner, every window ledge and every piece of furniture.

Web duty was the worst job to have on clean-up day.

"I can't do it, Raj," whispered his cousin Christopher. "I can't do webs. Do you know how long that takes?"

"Stick with me," said Raj. "I've got a plan."

His plan was volunteering for the second-worst job. They would clean out the haunted shack. By choosing the second-worst job, they avoided the very worst, and they didn't look lazy either. It was the best Raj could come up with.

The haunted shack was a small building behind the haunted mansion. Every year Uncle Dan hid a speaker inside that played screams and bloodcurdling laughter. It was decorated with plastic pumpkin lights. A skeleton popped out of a window every few minutes.

"Everybody to their stations!" announced Uncle Dan. The cousins rushed to their various jobs.

Rumour had it that the shack was the home of bugs and rats and maybe worse. But Raj didn't mind. "At least there's not miles and miles of cobwebs," said Raj as he pulled open the squeaky door.

He spoke too soon. As soon as he and Christopher stepped inside, they walked into a wall of sticky webbing.

"Ewwwww! I told you I didn't want to deal with webs," said Christopher.

"These shouldn't be here," said Raj. "Trick-or-treaters don't even come inside the shack on Halloween."

"Uncle Dan put these here on purpose," said Christopher. "He guessed we'd weasel out of web duty, like we did last year. He's trying to teach us a lesson." Christopher looked around for a stick or tool he could use to rip a path through the clingy material.

Raj fought his way inside. "Well, we're stuck with it now," he said. A thick web coiled around his legs. It was connected to the door, and as Raj trudged forward, the door was pulled shut behind him.

Christopher had had enough of the webs. As he headed back to the closed door, the webs seemed to grow thicker. More and more of them wrapped around his legs and arms. "I can hardly move," said Christopher.

"Mmmmphhfh!" Raj couldn't answer. Webbing was tightening around his face and chest like boa constrictors.

Christopher's arms were soon bound to his sides. "This is not going to work," he said.

A high, thin sound echoed through the air. The web was trembling.

Raj saw a dark shadow moving in the corner of the shack. Eight hairy arms reached out from a thick, round body. Eight eyes gleamed.

Click . . . Click . . .

"Spider!" Raj tried to shout. But it was no use. The webbing was too thick, too strong.

A bony jaw clicked in the darkness. *Click . . . Click . . . Click.* The eight eyes focused on the struggling boys. They had made a mess of the spider's lovely web. The creature decided it was time to clean up.

Click . . . Click . . .

Crunch.

DON'T READ THIS STORY AT MIDNIGHT!

Please. Not at midnight.

And yes, there's a reason for that. Midnight is the time I can count on you being asleep. Deep asleep. And that's important to me, because that's the only time I can slip out from underneath your bed without you seeing me.

Because if you saw me, well, the game's over.

You'd know right away I'm not human. Not with my ears at the bottom of my head and my eye – well, I don't want to get into all that.

So, if you are reading this at midnight, then please do me a favour. Do us both a favour. Put the book down. Turn out the lights. Try to sleep. At the very least, don't make any noise when you hear that slippery sound beneath you. It's just me.

Keep your eyes closed, too. If you are one of the curious types, don't say anything when you see that shadow crawling towards your door. Ignore it.

Oh, and whatever you do, do not – I repeat, do not – turn the lights back on.

I have a fear of sudden lights. And I can't predict my behaviour when it happens. Who knows what I would do. Like pounce or something. I hate to think about it. I'm pretty sure you wouldn't like it either.

Let's keep the lights out. The dark is a much happier place for me.

And if you do happen to fall asleep, then great. It's a win-win. My friend will have time to crawl out from under the bed, too.

FINGERS ON THE GLASS

The wind picked up suddenly, rolling across the countryside. A storm of swiftly falling snow swallowed up cars, trucks and buses, and their passengers.

Jada looked out of the car window. It was night and the snow was falling so heavily it was hard to see. She shifted into a more comfortable position in the backseat and returned to her video game.

"Bill, slow down. The road is pure ice," Jada's mother said through clenched teeth.

"It's not, and I'm barely going the speed limit," said her father. He glanced into the rear-view mirror. "How are you doing back there?"

"Fine," said Jada. Her head stayed down,

focused on her game. It was a new version of *Boyz from Otherworld.*

She wasn't worried about the snow, but it did seem to be taking longer to get home from her cousins' than usual. There were long stretches of country road with no traffic lights. Twice Jada could see cars in the ditch. Headlights angled crazily through the falling snowflakes.

One headlight caught her in the face. Jada blinked. Just before she did, she saw a strange shape on the side window. It looked like a boy's hand sliding down the wet, snowy glass. As if he was lying on the roof of the car and reaching down on Jada's side to grab the door handle.

She blinked again and the hand had gone.

What did her teacher call that? An afterimage. A shape or figure you might see after a bright glare of light. Whatever it was called, it was strange.

Jada kept playing. The car was dead quiet. The silence was broken only by a nervous gasp from her mother or a grunt from her father as he gazed through sheets of snow.

Then Jada heard another noise. It was a soft noise. It came from the window next to her. She saw it again. A boy's hand was plastered to the glass. At least, she thought it was a boy's hand. For some reason that was the idea that popped into her head. Maybe because of her video game about boys from an alien realm. But what a silly thought: a boy lying on the roof of the car, out in the snow.

Jada blinked, but this time the hand stayed there. The fingers began to move slowly, crawling down the glass.

"Dad," Jada said softly.

"Don't bother your father," said her mum. "He's trying to concentrate."

"What is it, honey?" her dad asked.

"Bill, watch the road," said her mother.

The hand had gone.

Jada looked down at her video game. She turned it off and set it on the seat next to her. She rubbed her eyes. She was getting tired. It had been a long night visiting her cousins, with too much birthday cake and ice cream and biscuits. She still felt full. Her warm stomach was making her sleepy.

The noise came again. A damp, spongy thump. This time it came from the other side of the car.

The small hand was reaching down from the roof. It moved like a wet spider down her father's window. Jada gasped.

A second hand reached down to join the first. They both slid down the window. Were they going to open her dad's door?

"Mum –" she began.

"Not now, Jada," her mum said sharply, not taking her eyes off the road.

"But –"

"I said, not now."

Jada took several deep breaths. She must be dreaming. How could anyone survive on the roof of the car in this weather? Why would they be out there, even if they could survive? It made no sense.

Jada saw more headlights up ahead. Another car in the ditch? She looked out of her window and immediately froze.

The boy's face was on the other side of the window, looking directly at her. His hands were braced on either side of his face. His mouth was open in a perfect O, as if he were screaming. But to Jada, all was silent, like an image on TV with the sound turned off.

After a moment, though, there was a scream. It was Jada's.

Her father, startled, turned the steering wheel. The car slid slightly on the icy road. Jada's mother yelled. Her dad braked and brought it to a swift, solid stop.

"What in the world?" he cried.

"Jada, what is the matter with you?" her mother demanded.

"A boy!" gasped Jada. "There's a boy out on our car. I saw him. I saw him!"

A terrified look clouded her mother's face.

"I'm not making it up," said Jada. "He's on the roof." Her voice broke. She tried hard not to cry.

Her mother glanced nervously at her husband. "Bill, what are you doing?" He had opened his door.

"There's nothing on our car," he said to Jada. "I'll show you." He stepped out into the blizzard and slammed the door shut.

They couldn't see him even one metre from the car. Her mother panicked. "Stay right here," she ordered Jada. Then she, too, opened her door and stepped out, swallowed up in a wall of blowing snow.

Jada waited a few minutes. Were her parents out there with the mysterious boy?

Fear turned her stomach to ice. Jada dashed out of the car. "Mum! Dad!" she cried. The headlights from their car showed only a wall of snow. "Mum!" she called again.

"We're over here, honey!" called her father.

Jada pulled her cap down over her hair. She pulled her collar tight around her neck. Then she leaned into the wind and snow and trudged towards them.

"Over here!" her dad called again.

Her parents were standing in the road about five metres from where they had stopped. A heavy oak tree, its branches weighed down with snow, had fallen across the road.

"Back in the car," said her dad. "We'll go back to Highway Three and drive around this mess."

When they reached the car, Jada's mum whispered to her. "If your dad hadn't stopped, we would have crashed right into that tree. I hate to think what would have happened."

"Talk about luck," said her dad, shaking his head.

Jada had her hand on the handle of her car door when she looked up. Some of the snow on the roof had been knocked off. The boot of the car had a clear path through the middle of its snow cover, as if a small body had slid down from the roof and onto the ground. And there, behind the car, was a trail of footprints running away. Jada watched the footprints slowly filling up with snow, disappearing into the blizzard.

When she returned to the backseat, Jada reached down. The video game player had gone. And the seat was wet with melting snow.

LEGENDS -
TRUE OR
FALSE

Tynan hated English tests, especially on Friday afternoons. But Mr Loup's tests were usually pretty easy. Tynan grabbed his pencil and started reading.

This test will concentrate on
the more important monsters
from our Legends unit.

Duh, thought Tynan.

1. Monsters are based on real,
   living creatures.

   True or False

Um, that wasn't so easy. Dragons were not based on living creatures, but things like zombies were.

Their legends came from real life – people who had been accidentally buried. People who had fainted or something like that, and then woke up and found themselves in a coffin and climbed out. The lucky ones did, anyway.

Tynan circled *True*.

> 2. Monsters are a symbol of our fears about the unknown.
>
> True or False

Tynan had no idea what that question meant. He thought it sounded like a clever question, so he'd better answer *True*.

> 3. Shape-shifters are a type of legendary monster.
>
> True or False

Shape-shifters were really creepy, Tynan remembered. Some of the old Viking warriors would wear the skins of animals they had killed. Then they turned into those same animals. Like bears or wolves. Tynan had once watched his uncle skin a bear he had shot. It looked cool, but Tynan couldn't imagine putting that bloody carcass around his shoulders. Ughh. And the smell! Tynan circled *True*.

4. Shape-shifters can
   disguise themselves as
   human beings.

   True or False

Easy one, thought Tynan. *True.* Ty looked up at Mr Loup standing in the corner. His teacher was watching the clock. He probably wanted to start the weekend just as much as his students did.

5. Your teacher is a shape-
   shifter.

   True or False

Tynan looked up again. Was Mr Loup smiling? It was one of his typical trick questions. Very funny. But then, as Tynan pretended to study the test, he watched under his lowered eyebrows. He thought the man's smile changed. It looked wider. He could see Mr Loup's teeth.

He'd circle *True* just for kicks. Mr Loup would find it funny.

6. If your teacher were a shape-shifter, he would survive by eating humans.

True or False

Ha ha! Totally disgusting, thought Tynan. But true. A werewolf was a kind of shape-shifter, and they ate humans.

7. With so many humans to eat in one classroom, a good method would be alphabetical order.

True or False

Tynan heard his classmates shifting in their chairs. A few people sniggered. Jill, the class geek, gasped. Mr Loup was still smiling. Tynan frowned at the question. If it *was* true, he was glad his last name was Zimmerman.

8. You wish your last name came at the end of the alphabet.

True or False

Tynan blinked. He looked up quickly and met Mr Loup's gaze. The teacher was smiling. He was also nodding slightly, as if he could read Tynan's mind.

A cold shudder ran down Tynan's body. What if that question was only on *his* test? What if the tests had been written specially for each student? Suddenly, Tynan felt like he needed the toilet. He was about to put his hand up, but he couldn't move. His feet were glued to the floor. His bottom was stuck to the chair.

Tynan's friend Kent shouted, "What's going on?"

Tynan looked quickly down at the next question.

> 9. Shape-shifters hypnotize their victims before they attack.
>
> True or False

That's what it is, he thought. *A joke.* Mr Loup was pranking them. Somehow he had hypnotized the entire class. That's why he had been holding that funny little crystal he kept on his desk. The sunlight from the window glittered on the crystal as Mr Loup turned it over and over in his hand.

Tynan wanted to laugh. No sound came from his throat. He tried to ask a question, but he couldn't speak.

As he stared at his teacher, he thought he heard the man's voice in his head. *Aren't you glad the test is almost over?* Tynan looked down at the paper.

```
10. You are glad the test is
    almost over.

    True or False
```

For the students whose last names begin with A through to G, you may now put your pencils down and follow me.

Tynan and half the other students were still frozen. They watched as their classmates at the front of the room slowly stood up and followed Mr Loup towards the window. He opened it in one swift move. He swung his legs over the sill. The students followed, one by one. In a few moments they had disappeared into the woods next to the school.

A wolf's howl echoed in the distance.

Tynan and the others all dropped their pens at the same time. They could move again.

Another howl came from the woods. Jill looked at Tynan with fear in her eyes. "Do you think this means we can skip the bonus question?" she asked.

THE
BALLOON

It looked like an ordinary balloon to Vance Green as it flew over his neighbourhood. Except for one thing . . .

Instead of drifting with the wind, the balloon was locked in an orbit. It seemed to be travelling in a circle above the houses and trees along Oak Street and Madison Lane.

The balloon was silent, but Vance and his friends made plenty of noise as they phoned and texted each other about it. "Over my house again," Vance shouted into his phone to his friend Rufus. He texted the same information to his other three friends, who were all watching the strange balloon from their various gardens.

"Same here!" shouted his friend Rufus.

"Heading this way again," texted Tonio.

"Vance," said his father, who was hosing off the patio furniture in their back garden. "Can you keep it down? You and your friends are always so loud!"

"It's that balloon, Dad," Vance said as he jumped up and down and pointed to the sky. "It's coming back. It keeps coming back!"

"Fine, it's a balloon," said his father, staring up and shielding his eyes with his hand. "Do you have to be so noisy about it? This used to be such a nice, quiet neighbourhood –"

"'Before you cute little kids got older.' Yeah, yeah, I know," interrupted Vance. His father reminded him of that at least once a day.

"I'm going inside," said his father, setting down the last patio chair. "I'm going to watch my cop show. At least that will be nice and quiet."

Vance felt his phone buzz in his pocket and pulled it out. "6TII TIME," texted Rufus.

"I thought it was 7," sent Irene.

While the sun set, Vance stood in his garden and kept watch. Again and again Vance saw the object float over the weathervane on the Greens' rooftop and then disappear past the elm trees next door. It followed the same orbit above the same few houses: Vance, Irene, Tonio, Gabe, Rufus, Vance.

Then something changed.

"It's lower," texted Tonio from across the street.

"RUNNING OUT OF AIR???" texted Gabe.

"IT'S BIG!!!!" shouted Rufus from next door.

"Rufus! Keep it down," said his mother.

Vance waited for the balloon to sail into view from Rufus's house next door. His friends were right. The balloon seemed larger and was definitely lower to the ground. The blue-violet sphere winked in the fading sunlight. It barely cleared the highest branches of the elm tree in Vance's yard. When Vance saw it earlier, he thought the balloon was a standard size, maybe 20 centimetres across. Now that it was floating closer, Vance guessed it was more like 60 centimetres across – possibly bigger.

"REALLY BIG!" texted Irene. "Maybe three metres across."

Huh? It isn't that big, thought Vance. It had floated out of sight just seconds ago.

"Hey Tonio," sent Vance. "How big do u think?"

Tonio didn't reply straight away like he usually did. A few minutes later, this message came: "Lower now. It's in my garden!"

"I'm coming over," sent Rufus.

Vance, too, had stuffed his phone into his pocket and headed across the quiet street. He saw Irene and Rufus running along either side of him. When they reached Tonio's garden, Gabe was already there.

"Where'd he go?" asked Rufus.

Gabe frowned. "I came right over," he said. "No one was here."

The four friends glanced quickly around the darkening lawn. They started shouting for Tonio, but Tonio's dad shouted out of the window telling them to be quiet.

"He just texted all of us," said Irene. "Where did he go?"

"And where's that crazy balloon?" asked Vance.

The garden was empty. Four heads tilted upwards, four pairs of eyes scanned the violet sky.

"There!" shouted Rufus. "It's back over my house again."

Hooting and screaming, each of them ran back to their own garden to track the strange object.

Vance stood behind his house again, stared up and waited. And waited.

"Rufus, where is it?" he texted.

Rufus didn't answer. Vance ran to the fence that separated their two gardens and peered over. Rufus had gone.

"I SEE IT!" came a message from Irene. "Rolling on the grass."

Vance turned quickly and ran to the other side of his garden. He pushed past the bushes and stepped into Irene's garden. He wanted to catch a close-up of the growing sphere.

Irene wasn't there. He called out for her a few times, but there was no answer. Instead, Irene's older sister Debbie stepped outside and looked at him. "What are you shouting about?" she demanded.

"Where's Irene?" Vance asked. He had a sick, cold feeling in the bottom of his stomach.

"How should I know?" said Debbie. She rolled her eyes and walked back into the house.

Vance's phone buzzed. He looked down and saw a smiley face with its tongue sticking out. Gabe!

"Gabe, u there?" texted Vance.

Gabe sent back: "Cool. It's rolling over the garden. Wonder where it's going."

A full minute went by.

Vance stopped texting and called Gabe on the phone. It rang a few times and then went to voicemail.

What's happening? thought Vance. He slowly left Irene's place and walked past the bushes into his own garden. His dad was standing there.

"Dad! Dad! That balloon –" Vance started.

His father interrupted him. "I was wondering where you were," he said. "I was afraid you were going to miss it."

Vance frowned. "Miss what?" he said.

His father smiled. "The balloon we ordered."

"Ordered?" said the boy.

"Well, I certainly couldn't afford it on my own," said his father. "All the parents chipped in. It's the best we could do."

Vance felt a cold breeze at his back. He turned slowly and saw the balloon rolling across the lawn towards them. It was huge – a dark sphere, almost as large as a hot-air balloon.

His dad nodded. "Maybe now we can have some peace and quiet around here. Just like it used to be. Make the neighbourhood a great place again."

The balloon rolled closer and closer without making a sound. All Vance could see was a wide, stretching blue-violet wall. It grew and grew . . .

"Dad!" shouted Vance.

The balloon rolled over the boy, and suddenly he had gone.

Vance's father stood in the garden alone. The man noticed something shining in the wet grass. He reached down and picked up Vance's phone. Then he took a deep breath. He listened to the faint chirp of crickets and a bird singing softly in a nearby tree.

"So peaceful again," he said.

Then he walked quietly back into his house. The balloon rose straight up into the night sky. It was silent, except for a few faint sounds from within the sphere. Sounds that someone might mistake for the noisy screams of children.

SHADOW SHOES

Daphne was too old to still believe there were monsters under her bed. But for the past three nights, she'd heard noises down there. Bumps and thumps, as if something had been dropped onto the wooden floor. She was convinced it wasn't an alligator or a zombie, but that still didn't make her brave enough to peer under the bed.

Whenever she heard the noise, Daphne checked the clock on her nightstand. The glowing numerals always displayed 10:01.

One night, before Daphne turned her light off, she set her alarm clock to ring a few minutes before ten o'clock. When she awoke, she lay in bed. She pulled the covers up to her chin and waited for the noise. If nothing happened, she'd know it had been a dream. Slowly the minutes passed, then . . .

Thump! Whump!

It was not a dream. Daphne reached over carefully and turned her light back on. She slowly slid her legs over the side of the bed. Her bare feet slipped down to the cold wood floor. She sat on the edge of the bed for a full minute.

This is stupid, she told herself. *There are no monsters under the bed!*

Daphne knelt down and lifted the covers that draped from her bed to have a look.

She gasped. She never expected this: a pair of shoes. Shoes that were not hers. Daphne pulled them out for a closer look.

Even though Daphne's bedside light was on, it was hard to see the shoes. They appeared fuzzy, as if her eyes were still sleepy. Their shape reminded her of running shoes. It was hard to make out their colour, but Daphne guessed they were a deep midnight blue. Her favourite colour. Pale, glowing stars decorated the sides of each shoe.

Most importantly, they looked exactly her size.

Daphne sat on the edge of the bed and tried them on. Why not? Maybe her mum and dad had put them there as some kind of early birthday present.

When the girl slipped them on, she felt relaxed. The shoes fitted perfectly. Even without socks on, they felt warm and soft. Now she could see the shoes clearly. They were indeed a lovely shade of midnight blue, with twinkling stars on the sides. And as the stars pulsed with a glowing orange and gold, the bedside light went out.

The girl didn't care. She could still see by the pale light of the stars.

She had never owned a pair of shoes this comfortable before. The strangely wonderful feeling travelled through her feet and legs and into the rest of her body.

Daphne stood up and took a few steps. She stepped into a rectangle of moonlight at the window. Suddenly, Daphne had an urge to walk outside. She ran into the hallway – then quickly stopped. She looked back at her bedroom door. It was closed. She hadn't touched it as she had raced into the hall. How did she get out here?

Daphne reached for the door handle. The tips of her fingers felt a strange coolness, but that was all. Her fingers seemed to pass through the handle, as if it were only a shadow.

Some people might feel frightened by that. Daphne was thrilled. She ran downstairs, the shoes barely making a whisper on the steps. When she got to the back door, Daphne reached out. Again, her hand passed through the handle. The girl took a deep breath and made a bold decision.

She closed her eyes and walked forward. In a few seconds, she felt cold air brushing against her body. Daphne opened her eyes and found she was standing outside in the alleyway, less than a metre from her back door.

Daphne ran down the alley, her shoes silently helping her along. In a few blocks, she entered the nearby park. Thick black shadows filled the spaces beneath the heavy trees. Spots of moonlight dappled the grass and walkways like small silver coins. Before tonight, Daphne would never have walked through the park alone, and never in the dark. But her new confidence chased away all fear. She wasn't afraid of the shadows.

Daphne was a shadow herself.

The girl spent the next few hours running through the park and the nearby streets, testing her new powers. She passed through streetlights and postboxes and parked cars. A stray dog ran up to her and barked. Daphne bent down and tried to pet the animal, but her hand passed through his head. The dog fled, yipping as if stung by bees.

Daphne looked up at the clock tower in the park. It was almost twelve. A chill shook her shoulders, and somehow Daphne knew that she had to get back by midnight. *Just like Cinderella*, she thought.

Daphne quickly headed home. A strong breeze blew rubbish and newspapers into her path, but she walked through them all.

Back in her room, Daphne reluctantly removed the mysterious shoes, placing them gently on the floor. The digits on her bedside clock had reached twelve. A *thump* sounded. And the shoes had gone.

So there are *rules*, she thought.

The next day at school, Daphne thought of nothing but the shoes. The hours dragged by until that night, when once again she heard the thump of the shoes, bent down to grab them, and raced outside to play in the shadows.

The next few nights, Daphne followed this
routine. She put on her new shoes at 10:01. Then
she drifted through her house and neighbourhood
as an unseen shadow, returning to her room just
before midnight.

Some nights she watched people eating at
restaurants, floating through the windows to listen
in on their conversations. She slipped through
the walls of apartments to see how other people
spent their evenings. Most people were boring, she
decided. They simply sat around, watching TV or
their phones, or talking about their day, or doing
homework.

As the nights passed, Daphne grew bolder. She
travelled further from her neighbourhood, and
once even drifted onto a bus. She sat next to
strangers, watched passengers sleep, read books
over their shoulders and saw them pick their cars
or noses when they thought no one could see them.
A few times, Daphne laughed out loud. No one
seemed to hear her.

On these nights when she was exploring, she had
to remind herself to keep checking the time. She
worried that if her shoes disappeared at midnight,
she might also vanish if she were still wearing
them.

I suppose I could just take them off if I needed to, she thought. *Though I'd have to walk home barefoot.*

Daphne experimented. While she stood in the shadowy park one night, she stepped out of the shoes. She gazed down. The shoes looked fuzzy, but they were still there. Everything else looked the same. The trees, the benches, the bins.

But Daphne felt different. She felt extremely tired, drained of all energy.

She barely had enough strength to put the shoes back on. As soon as she did, a flood of confidence surged through her body.

Daphne felt like a superhero.

It had been a week since she discovered the shadowy shoes. It was late, almost midnight. She was walking slowly through the park on her way back home.

I should probably take the shoes off, she told herself. *Just in case.*

Daphne bent down to slip off the shoes. They wouldn't budge. She sat down on a bench and pulled at the shoes. Her feet had swelled with all her walking. Now the shoes were too tight.

The girl panicked. She looked up at the clock tower. One minute to midnight.

She yanked the shoes, but they stayed firmly on her feet.

Daphne looked around the park. She was starting to worry. Surely there was someone who'd help her. But she was alone. Then she spied a tree root sticking above the ground. An old oak at the edge of the park had roots growing above the grass. Maybe she could wedge her foot against one of them while she pulled off the shoes.

Daphne ran across the park. A dog, the same stray as before, burst down the street and began barking at her again.

Daphne turned to look.

She should have watched where she was going. Daphne's left foot hit one of the roots and she tripped.

Her shoe slipped off as she fell. She extended her arms to catch herself. But her shadowy body was passing straight through the old tree trunk. Then both shoes fell off, grew blurry and dark, and then disappeared. Daphne screamed in pain, then blacked out.

The next morning a woman who was on her way to work noticed something odd about the tree at the edge of the park. She stared, then smiled to herself and shook her head. She could have sworn that an imprint in the bark looked like a young girl's face. It was amazing what you could see in nature. She took out her phone and snapped a photo. She'd have to share it with her friends.

The woman hurried on, her shoes striking solidly against the pavement.

ABOUT THE AUTHOR

Michael Dahl, the author of the Library of Doom and Troll Hunters series, is an expert on fear. He is afraid of heights (but he still flies). He is afraid of small, enclosed spaces (but his house is crammed with over 3000 books). He is afraid of ghosts (but that same house is haunted). He hopes that by writing about fear, he will eventually be able to overcome his own. So far it is not working. But he is afraid to stop. He claims that, if he had to, he would travel to Mount Doom in order to throw in a dangerous piece of jewellery. Even though he is afraid of volcanoes. And jewellery.

ABOUT THE ILLUSTRATOR

Xavier Bonet is an illustrator and comic-book artist who resides in Barcelona. Experienced in 2D illustration, he has worked as an animator and a background artist for several different production companies. He aims to create works full of colour, texture and sensation, using both traditional and digital tools. His work in children's literature is inspired by magic and fantasy as well as his passion for art.

MICHAEL DAHL TELLS ALL

Someone once asked J.K. Rowling how she came up with "Hogwarts", the name of the wizarding school in her famous Harry Potter series. She couldn't remember. A friend then asked her, sometime later, "Do you remember the first time we saw them?", "Saw what?" Rowling asked. Hogwarts turned out to be a kind of lily that Rowling and her friend had seen at a botanical garden, and the world-famous author had forgotten all about them. Ideas are like that. They come from experiences and events and then hide in your memory like prairie dogs down a hole. Then, without warning, they pop out and a story takes shape.

STUCK

Spiders don't bother me, but their webs do. Hate 'em. I really don't like how they feel against my face when I run into one. I park my car in the garage, and there must be a whole family of spiders living in there. Once, I left the window in the car open overnight, and the next morning a web was already stretching across the dashboard. Those little monsters are fast. Imagine what a giant-sized one could do.

DON'T READ THIS STORY AT MIDNIGHT!

I like stories that have warnings as titles. And I have never gotten over the idea that there is something under my bed at night. Even as an adult, I think about what could be down there. An alligator? A zombie? Something worse?

FINGERS ON THE GLASS

This story has been pinging around my brain for a long time. As a child, riding in the backseat of the car at night, before video games and phone apps, I often stared out of the dark windows. I imagined all kinds of things out there. Things that were just out of sight . . . perhaps on the roof or the boot of the car. When I was 11 years old, my cousins and I watched the classic *Twilight Zone* episode about the gremlin on the wing of the aeroplane. Yikes! That show not only scared me even more about flying, but it gave me a healthy respect for what's on the other side of windows. Especially windows on moving vehicles. Now that I've gotten this story out of my head and written it down, I hope dark windows won't bother me so much.

LEGENDS – TRUE OR FALSE

This story started as a challenge I gave myself. Could I write a scary tale that would be in the form of an exam? A test in an English lesson? Tests are only scary if you don't know the answers, right? But what if it's even more frightening when you *do* know the answers? I hadn't written a werewolf story in a long time either, so somehow that got in the mix, too.

THE BALLOON

Balloons seem harmless, which is why I wanted to use one in a scary tale. Authors like doing that, "topsy-turvying" people or objects or events that seem normal and innocent. Also, years ago when I was quite young, my dad and I would watch *The Prisoner* on TV. It was a strange adventure/spy/science fiction show about prisoners of a seemingly quiet seaside town. If any of the prisoners tried to escape, however, a strange white balloon came out of nowhere and tracked them down. I suppose I've never forgotten that unnerving white sphere bouncing along the shore, chasing some poor person until . . .

SHADOW SHOES

Two of my favourite comic-book heroes were Invisible Kid and Phantom Girl. They had the powers I always wanted: to turn invisible and walk through walls. Imagine what you'd see and hear. All secret stuff, mostly. You could hear what your friends or parents said when you weren't around. You could walk inside locked places like bank vaults or prisons or zoo cages and have cool adventures. Of course, something would probably go wrong. After all, superpowers and magical objects come with rules, and those rules should not be broken. Ask Harry Potter. Or Phantom Girl. Or poor Daphne in this story. I got the name Daphne from a Greek myth about a young girl who turns into, what else? A tree.

GLOSSARY

carcass dead body of an animal

cauldron large metal pot used for cooking over an open fire

confidence feeling or belief that you can succeed

headlight bright light at the front of a vehicle that allows the driver to see ahead in the dark

hypnotize put someone in a state in which the person appears to be asleep but can still hear and see and respond to suggestions and questions

legend story handed down from earlier times

moonless lacking the light of the moon

pounce jump forward and grab something suddenly

predict say what will happen in the future

realm kingdom

rumour story that is spread by word of mouth but that may not be true

sphere solid round form like that of a basketball or globe

werewolf in myth, a person who changes for periods of time into a wolf

DISCUSSION QUESTIONS

1. In the story "The Balloon", Vance and his friends are taken by a mysterious balloon. Why do you think they were taken? Were their parents involved? Use examples from the text to discuss the possibilities.

2. In "Fingers on the Glass", Jada isn't sure whether she is imagining the boy outside her car window. Have you ever been spooked by something in your imagination? Talk about what it was and why it was scary.

3. Imagine you are Daphne in the story "Shadow Shoes". Do you hesitate before putting on the mysterious shoes? Why or why not? Talk about your decision using examples from the text.

WRITING PROMPTS

1. I am terrified of spider webs, which is where my story "Stuck" came from. What frightens you? Try writing a story about it.

2. Imagine there is a monster like the one in "Don't Read This Story at Midnight!" living under your bed. Write a scene in which you meet the monster for the first time.

3. In "Legends – True or False", we hear about the legend of shape-shifters. Think of a legend you've learned about in a book or film or from a friend and write a couple of paragraphs about the story.

MICHAEL DAHL'S

REALLY SCARY STORIES